Baby gets the Zapper

Ted DeWan

Picture Corgi Books

BABY
GETS THE ZAPPER
A CORGI BOOK 0552 547077

Published in Great Britain by Corgi Books,
an imprint of Random House Children's Books

First published in 2001 by Doubleday Children's Books
This edition published 2002

1 3 5 7 9 10 8 6 4 2

Copyright © 2001 Ted Dewan

Designed by Ian Butterworth

Corgi Books are published by Random House Children's Books,
61-63 Uxbridge Road, London W5 5SA,
a division of The Random House Group Ltd,
in Australia by Random House Australia (Pty) Ltd,
20 Alfred Street, Milsons Point, Sydney, NSW 2061, Australia,
in New Zealand by Random House New Zealand Ltd,
18 Poland Road, Glenfield, Auckland 10, New Zealand,
and in South Africa by Random House (Pty) Ltd,
Endulini, 5A Jubilee Road, Parktown 2193, South Africa

THE RANDOM HOUSE GROUP Limited Reg. No. 954009
www.kidsatrandomhouse.co.uk

A CIP catalogue record for this book is available
from the British Library.

Printed in Singapore

For Pandora,
who
changed
everything

Look.

Look what Baby's got.

Baby's got
the Zapper.

Baby doesn't like what's on TV.

Now see
what's on TV.

ZAP!

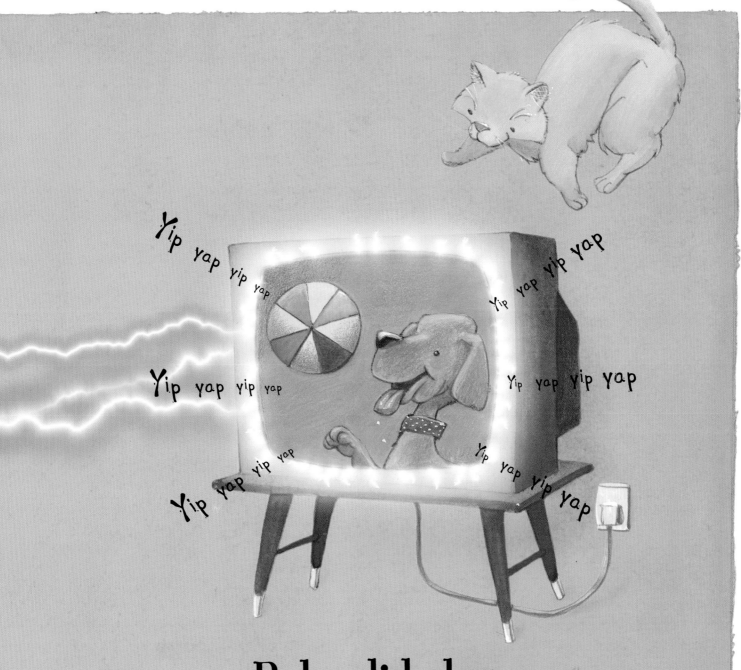

Baby did that.

Look at those toys all over the floor.

ZAP!

Twinkle twinkle
little star
how I wonder
what you are

Now those toys can
play music!

Baby did that.

What's that cat playing with?

Baby
climbs in . . .

floats through the window...

and zooms
out into
the night.

ZAP!

Hey, that's enough now, Baby.

Oh no, Baby.
What are you doing to
the moon?

ZAP!

Now it's a great big cookie!

Naughty Baby!
Greedy Baby!
Stop right now!

Oh no! Tipping over! Baby's falling down.

Down

down

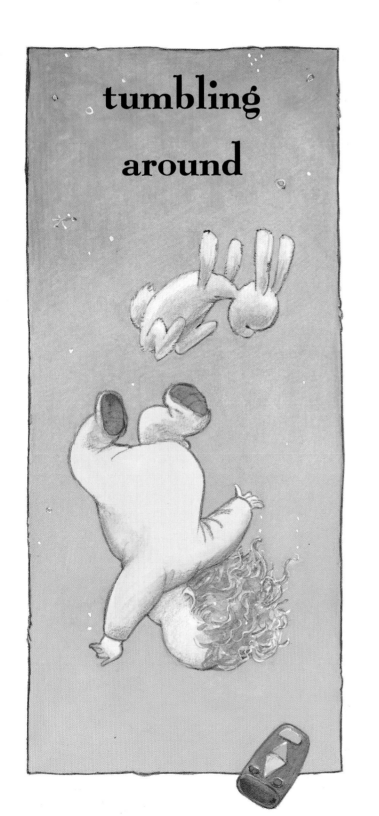

tumbling
around

down
to the
ground.

WHUMP! Just in time . . .

for a splashy
bath . . .

a bedtime story . . .

and a lullaby.

Look. Mama gets
the Zapper.

ZAP!

Good night,
Baby.

Mama did that.